MAX AND MARLA

ALEXANDRA BOIGER

G. P. PUTNAM'S SONS
An Imprint of Penguin Group (USA)

To Vanessa and Andrea
with great love and thanks
for being my inspiration
and foundation.

G. P. PUTNAM'S SONS
Published by the Penguin Group
Penguin Group (USA) LLC
375 Hudson Street
New York, NY 10014

USA | Canada | UK | Ireland | Australia
New Zealand | India | South Africa | China
penguin.com
A Penguin Random House Company

Library of Congress Cataloging-in-Publication Data is available upon request.
Manufactured in China by RR Donnelley Asia Printing Solutions Ltd.
ISBN 978-0-399-17504-6
1 3 5 7 9 10 8 6 4 2

Design by Annie Ericsson. Text set in Brandon Grotesque.
The art for this book was rendered in watercolor and ink on Fabriano paper, then
scanned and further overworked in Photoshop by adding spot textures and colors.

MAX and MARLA are best friends.

They are Olympians. Real-life,
honest to goodness, cross your heart,
W-i-n-t-e-r O-l-y-m-p-i-c-s Olympians.

Wait, you don't believe me?

Just watch.

Preparation is key.
And these two are very good at preparing.

"Ready, Marla?" asks Max.

"Here we come!"

I told you! They are true Olympians.

Ready. Set. **GO!**

"We are not going anywhere, Marla."

Oh boy. Our Olympians face technical difficulties.

"We must tend to this immediately."

True Olympians never give up.

Marla and Max get to it right away. Taking care of
your equipment takes time and it is very important.

As is teamwork.
"Marla, could you hand me the wax, please?
. . . Marla?"

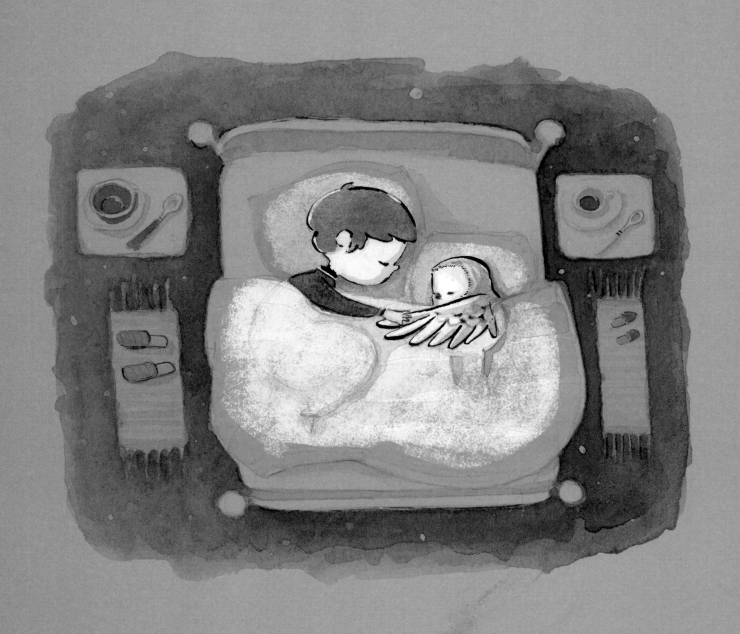

Tomorrow will be a new day.

Today the team has added a number of improvements to their routine.

The equipment double check.
Max: "Okay?"
Max: "Okay!"
Marla: Thumbs up!

"Here we come again!"

Just look at them! They are fearless.
Prepared for the unexpected.

True Olympians never give up.

"Marla, we must take a sick day," says Max.
"Taking care of yourself is important.
Probably most important of all."

The two athletes are fully recovered.
"Look, Marla," says Max, "this time we are
going to prepare for absolutely everything."

Any wind today? No.
Perfect weather conditions.

Preparation really is THE key.

Obstacles are turned into victories.

Max and Marla are true Olympians.